BESSEL STATION
Blues

A Science Fiction/Mystery Novella

REBECCA M. SENESE

ALSO BY REBECCA M. SENESE

BESSEL STATION
Blues

A Science Fiction/Mystery Novella

REBECCA M. SENESE

RFAR PUBLISHING
TORONTO, CANADA

Published 2021 by RFAR Publishing
Toronto, Canada
https://www.RFARPublishing.com

Trade paperback edition and electronic editions designed
by Rebecca M. Senese in Vellum Press.

Cover Design copyright © (2021) by
RFAR Publishing

Cover art copyright ©
Wampa76/DepositPhotos.com

Paperback ISBN: 978-1-927603-44-4

BESSEL STATION
Blues

A Science Fiction/Mystery Novella

1

Being a private detective on the Bessel Station wasn't all it was cracked up to be. Most days I was lucky to make enough credits to let me grab a meal at one of the food distributors on O level. If not, I had to settle for the recycled sludge that came out of the old food recycler that perched on the edge of my small desk.

The recycler had definitely seen better days. The squat, retangular body, a foot and a half long and barely eight inches wide, was dented on both sides and the paint had long faded to reveal the flat metal form. The dents had come from an overly annoyed perp. They fit the top of his head perfectly.

The recycler had never quite worked right since.

The buttons on the top were faded as well but it didn't matter what configuration I tried to punch in, I would always get the same old sludge.

The sludge was nutritious and I could live on it but it had as much taste as my ex-husband.

Too bad my ex-husband was the senior security chief on the station and one of my largest clients.

Mother had always told me to finish my doctorate and

become a lawyer for the Planetary Alliance. I could have worked my way up to being a magistrate, maybe even become a senator. But that would have entailed being stuck in bright white offices filled with bright holo screens, wearing immaculate suits and conference links along with the latest in seasonal hairstyles.

I bet if I'd done that I would have my own chef instead of relying on the culinary skills of some third-rate food recycler on a second-rate space station.

But I'd always hated white walls and I preferred keeping my head shaved to avoid the hassle of dealing with a hairstyle that might cause a problem in zero gee.

And suits gave me hives. Just like the security uniform had.

Another of the reasons my marriage hadn't lasted.

So all I had was my little hovel of an office. Steel-grey walls showing every weld. The narrow metal desk that I'd scrounged from the recycling plant. One leg was too short until I shoved the folded remnants of my marriage license under it.

My aforementioned food recycler perched on the left side of the desk, still steaming from discharging my most recent mug of coffee. It might be crap at creating food with actual taste but it could brew coffee just how I liked it. Black and strong enough to strip a layer of skin off the roof of my mouth.

I leaned back in my deluxe Self-Chair. It was the only thing in my entire office worth a solid amount of credits, including me. I'd spent every credit from the divorce settlement on it. It was a large blob shape until I moved toward it and then it shaped itself to whatever I needed. A desk chair for work. A recliner for holo work when I was surfing the datastreams. A bed when I needed to sleep. It would even flow into an emergency bubble in case of depressurization in the station and could be a life pod, complete with a rudimentary engine for navigation and life support if necessary.

It was more supportive and more useful than my husband had ever been.

Fortunately, I'd never had to test the life pod aspect of it.

The steam from my mug diminished enough that I could lift it to my nose without singeing myself. I inhaled the warm, rich smell of coffee. Ahh, elixir of life!

As I leaned back in my Self-Chair, it stiffened to support my back. I began lowering my left hand holding the mug. The left arm of the chair expanded and flattened, becoming a small side table for my coffee.

That always made my smile. God, I loved this chair.

I just had to figure out how I was going to afford the upgrade.

I'd heard about it a few weeks ago. There was an upgrade to both the physical set up and the software that allowed you to liaise directly with the chair, turning it more into an intelligent assistant than just a chair.

I'd already given it the nickname of Robby. Just thinking about having Robby do more than help me sleep or connect to the datastreams made me salivate. With enough awareness, I could assign it work on the datastreams while I did other jobs.

Maybe I could even get out from under, afford two meals a day at the food distributors on O level. Hell, maybe I could even replace my food recycler and get one that understood spices.

But first, I had to find a case that would earn me enough to pay for Robby's upgrade. Right now, the Self-Chair was only smart enough to give me a side table when I needed it. I would never be able to assign it to work on the datastreams without supervision.

The trouble with Bessel Station, like all space stations, was that the Planetary Alliance only allowed their security to work legitimately on stations. Fortunately, most of the time, the security forces on stations didn't have enough staff to handle everything so they farmed work out to small time operators like me.

I existed in a legal grey area. The PA turned a blind eye to private detectives on station as long as we stayed out of trouble and didn't do anything to attract notice.

Unfortunately, the only jobs that let me stay out of trouble and not attract notice barely paid enough credits for a meal at the food distributors after paying my rent.

If I wanted to upgrade Robby I was going to have to get a case that made some noise.

Just not enough to piss off the PA.

Which really meant not enough to piss off my ex-husband.

That was gonna be some neat trick.

I took another sip of coffee, savouring the strong kick of caffeine. I was just about to set it down on the chair arm table when a soft tap sounded at the door.

I triggered the right chair arm and leaned over, keeping my voice low.

"Analysis scan beyond door."

My office was located at an end junction on T level, far enough from the lift that I could afford the rent and far enough that it would take precious minutes for any security to get here if there was a problem. Most offices on T level were one person shops like me, barely eeking out a living but that wouldn't stop a thug from trying to smash in and steal the passcode to my credit stash. I'd learned very early on to never open the door without checking with Robby first.

The little sensor light on the tip of the right arm flashed green.

"Analysis complete. Bipedal humanoid lifeform. Negative power trace. Negative tools larger than two inches." Robby's flat voice matched my volume.

Good. No plaz-gun and no knife or tool to hit with. I had programmed Robby to scan for anything bigger than two inches to make sure no one could sneak anything in.

The soft tap sounded again. This time I felt more willing to answer it.

"Door open," I called.

The door clicked and hissed open. A thin, balding man stepped in. He wore grey overalls over a dark blue, long-sleeved top. The sleeves were rolled up to reveal narrow forearms poked with nutrient valves, the kind you normally saw on space workers. But these valves were old, the seals turning yellow with age.

As he stopped in front of my desk, he tucked his chin in, giving me a slight bow. He had blond hair that was thinning at the top, retreating from his forehead like a reluctant army.

"Can I help you, mister...?" I asked.

"Claymore, ma'm," he said. His voice had a rough burr to it, like he'd spend years yelling so loud that his vocal cords were damaged. "Roy Claymore."

I nodded. "Mr. Claymore."

"Yer a detective," he continued. "I heard 'bout you in the docks."

I gave another nod. That made sense. A lot of my spill-over work from security involved background checks on dock workers. Tedious, mind-numbing, yet essential work. No one wanted to take a chance on an incident like the sabotage and riot on Fairfell Station twenty years ago. It did say something about me that my ex had the confidence in my work to give me most of the dock background checks.

Or he hated me.

"I wanna hire you," Claymore said.

I took another sip of coffee to hide my surprise. I didn't get many walk-in clients. I couldn't even be sure he was one.

"What's the job?" I asked.

He frowned, heavy brows drawing forward above his eyes darkening the shadows. His shoulders hunched a little more.

"I got credits," he said. His tone sounded wounded, like I doubted him.

"That's good," I said. "But I still need to know what the job is first. I'm not taking any job until I know that."

His lips thinned. His body tensed. For a moment I thought he was going to turn around and stalk out the door. Then he sagged, all tension draining away until he almost hunched halfway over my desk.

"I want you to find someone," he said.

His voice was so low I could barely hear him. Still, I didn't lean forward. Once I'd had an angry client make a grab for me when I got too close. He'd lived but I'd broken two nails in the process of taking him down. Manicures were damned expensive and not in my budget.

"Who do you want me to find?" I asked.

He mumbled, tucking his chin into his neck until he was staring at the top of my desk.

"Speak up," I snapped. "I can't help you if I can't hear you."

He jumped, his head jerking up. I saw a flash of fear in his eyes then it was gone. He glanced around my office then back at me.

Then he shook his head.

"No, never mind. I made a mistake."

He started backing away, stumbling as his boots got caught up in each other.

The poor man was terrified.

I pushed up from Robby, holding my hands out Claymore. "Wait, Mr. Claymore. No one can hear you in here. I sweep the office for listening devices daily."

He stopped just inside the door. His hand twitched at his side as if he wanted to grab for the door but some powerful force was stopping him.

"Every day?" he asked.

"Yes," I said. "It's very thorough. Please, won't you sit down."

I tapped the edge of the desk and my single guest stool slid out from underneath. The desk sagged a little toward that side. Usually the stool helped hold the desk up but it would be okay for a few minutes.

Hopefully.

Claymore hesitated. His hands still twitched at his sides. I sat back down into Robby, moving with slow, deliberate motions. I gestured to the food recycler.

"Would you like some coffee?" I asked. "It's good and strong."

For a moment, I thought Claymore was still going to make a run for it. I could almost hear the clang of his boots on the metal floor of the hallway. But instead, he let out a sigh and shuffled toward the stool.

"Coffee, yeah," he said.

As he moved closer to the stool, I turned my attention to the food recycler and busied myself making coffee. I had an extra mug, actually clean, and I set it under the recycler's liquid shoot. The recycler made a slight whirling noise then began to belch out dribbles of coffee. After a moment, the rich, heavy scent of strong fresh coffee filled the air.

Out of the corner of my eye, I surreptitiously watched Claymore as he sat down. His posture was a mix of tension and relief. The stool didn't have a back so he couldn't lean back on it. That might account for the tension, but somehow I didn't think it did. Whoever Claymore wanted me to find and whatever he was afraid of seemed to war for attention inside him.

I had to give him enough time to decide to tell me but not enough to decide to make a run for it.

Fortunately, at that moment, the food recycler finished disgorging the coffee.

I slid the white mug across the scuffed surface of my desk

until it rested before Claymore. Steam drifted lazily out of the top of the mug. I watched Claymore inhale it.

"It's the real thing," I said. "I use only the best algorithms. There's no skimping on coffee."

That earned me the shadow of a smile across his narrow face. He wrapped his long fingers around the mug and lifted it to his lips. A sip seemed to relax him even more. He took a second mouthful before setting the mug down and lifting his gaze to me. From the firm set of his jaw, I could tell he'd made a decision.

"I want you ta find my son," he said. "RJ. Roy Junior."

I nodded, made a gesture for him to go on.

"He's a freelancer on the docks," Claymore said. He dropped his gaze and picked up the coffee mug again. His shoulders tensed.

A freelancer on the docks. A lot of implications in that single sentence. Had Roy Junior not qualified for the guild? Had he been kicked out for negligence? Criminal activity? Maybe not enough to be charged or not enough evidence for court, but enough to lose him his position? Or did he prefer the shady side of the docks?

Was that what was scaring Claymore?

He didn't seem inclined to volunteer any further information. I was going to have to pry it out of him.

"Did RJ have a regular position before?" I asked.

Claymore's fingers tightened around the mug, the knuckles blanching white.

Got it in one.

"Stewards had it in for 'im," Claymore mumbled. He had his head bowed, addressing the coffee mug.

I let my left hand drop onto the surface of my desk, palm slapping lightly. The sound made Claymore flinch but he did look up.

"I don't care about your son's priors," I said. "That's not my job. If I take this, my job is to find him and that's all. But I need to know everything to do it. The good and the bad. I don't care what they are, I just need to know."

Claymore let out a breath.

"Okay," he said. "RJ had been in the guild. He was always impatient with the politics of it, and his impatience cost him his papers."

Impatience. Right. It probably hadn't been RJ's impatience so much as some of the ships who decided they could skirt the system with a few well-placed payments. Except maybe RJ hadn't been inclined to share or had been saddled with a straight guild stewart rather than the usual kind who was willing to bend the rules, for a price.

Either way, RJ had lost his guild membership and was now freelance. A tougher, more dangerous, but potentially lucrative venture.

And somehow the danger had gotten to him before the lucrative part.

Claymore had to be prepared for that.

"Before we go on, I have to know how far you want to take this," I said.

Claymore lifted his chin. The scrawny muscles on the sides of his neck flexed as his shoulders stiffened.

"I know what yer asking," he said. "And yes, if he's dead, I wanna know that too."

His voice broke. He blinked away the moisture in his eyes.

I nodded, straightened the blotter on top of my desk to give him a moment to gain control. When I glanced back up, his eyes were clear, his features hardened.

"Okay," I said "Let's get started. Where did RJ live?"

2

The single room down on F level wasn't the worst I'd seen but it was far from the best. It was a single ten by seven pod room, wall-furnished, meaning all the furniture folded into the walls. All of it was dumb though. Nothing as sophisticated as Robby. Convenient, but it didn't really allow for personalized decoration. Still, RJ had done what he could with the place.

The walls were brushed metal with gouges where the individual pieces of furniture unfolded and scratched the surface. The single bed was still unfolded in the far corner. From the wrinkles in the sheets I could tell that RJ probably never folded it back up although it took up most of the space.

A set of two metal shelves were unfolded on the wall beside the bed. The top one held a variety of canned and packaged food, neatly arranged and grouped by what went together. The second shelf contained a few trinkets, the kind of thing a lot of dockers had, bits of metal or stone, given to them by spacers, souvenirs from other worlds.

But at the end of the shelf, RJ had a couple of items that surprised me.

Real, physical, hardback books.

It had been years since I'd seen a physical book. Few would bother to use up their weight and space allotment on a space ship for books.

Yet RJ had four, no, five books on his shelf.

Curious.

I slid along the side of the bed. There was maybe a foot of space so I wouldn't smack my head against the metal shelves. In the faintly metallic, recycled air, I could almost smell the musty paper scent of the books as I came face to face with them. They looked well worn, the fabric creased from use. A variety of burgundy, dark brown, and, even one navy blue, covers. Gold letters faded and chipped.

Ancient classics from Earth. Alice in Wonderland. Edgar Allan Poe. Shakespeare. Selected works of Stephen King. The bible.

Not at all what I expected from a freelance space docker.

Maybe I was going to have to change my assumptions about RJ or at the very least, keep an open mind.

I almost reached up for one of the books then stopped myself. It wasn't an official station investigation but there was still no sense in contaminating anything.

My trusty bottle of gel covering still had enough in it for use in this room. I slathered it onto my hands and waited the requisite ten seconds. Within that time, the gel solidified on my hands, creating a smooth, non-contaminating finish. More ecofriendly than any set of gloves. They didn't leave any kind of trace on anything and could easily be removed with water and some vigorous scrubbing. The friction and water caused the gel to dissolve with no more effect than soap down the drain and on a space station, every little bit help.

I tapped my fingers together. No stickiness. The gel had solidified.

Now I reached up for the books without fear of smearing my fingerprints on them or destroying any trace on the books themselves.

The books were all well used. The pages flipped easily, filling the air with the pungent scent of paper and ink. Or maybe I was imagining it. I wasn't sure I'd seen more than one book at a time in twenty years.

Some of the pages were dog-eared, especially in the Stephen King. Lines underlined, or marked at the side of the page. It made me think of researching and writing essays. Had RJ gone to a university or taken classes? I would have to ask Claymore.

All of the books were marked up. RJ certainly didn't believe in keeping them pristine. I had known some collectors who would have had fits over the many scribbles in the margins.

Had he been researching? The scribbles didn't even look like words to me, just dashes and dots mostly. Wiggly lines.

What kind of class would cause that kind of homework?

No English class I'd ever heard of.

The space on my back between my shoulder blades began to itch, the way it always did when something didn't make sense.

Exactly what kind of space docker was this RJ?

Had Claymore told me everything? The itch on my back became more pronounced.

Maybe the real question was had Claymore told me anything true?

I'd taken him at his word but I hadn't done any biometrics scan on him to determine if he was lying. Security on the station used all those fancy tricks but I didn't. Most of my clients were lying about something. As long as they gave me the information for the job, I didn't care.

But this time...

There was something really strange going on. It wasn't just the books. Even with its somewhat dingy appearance, this entire room felt staged. Maybe RJ did live here but it didn't have the feel of a permanent residence.

I focused in closer. The sheets on the bed, although wrinkled, looked relatively new. If RJ was really a space docker they should have been faded and worn.

The cans of food on the shelf. Too neat and too new. I picked up two at random and checked the expiry dates. Both over a year to go.

They'd been bought recently.

More staging.

I even moved over to the walls, poking at the scratches.

Fresh. Recently made.

This entire room was a set up.

Why?

Was someone setting me up? For what? I didn't have powerful enough enemies to go to these lengths or with this imagination. Most of my enemies would have settled for a punch to the stomach.

The only thing that felt authentic in this room were the books. Somehow they were the key.

I jerked upright. My shoulders clicked.

Of course.

The key.

The squiggles, the dashes, the dots. Not doodles or mistakes.

Codes.

Sweat trickled down the sides of my torso. I felt my body begin to tremble.

It was smarter than I was.

Time to get the hell out of here.

Give Claymore his retainer back. Refuse the job. Walk away.

But was it already too late?

If anyone was surveilling this room, they would have seen me go in. I was already compromised. Already involved.

There might be no backing away from this.

Dammit.

If that was the case, I couldn't just leave empty-handed.

I grabbed the Stephen King and jammed it under my jacket. Heading for the door, I took a last look around. Everything was in place. The messed up bedsheets. The remaining books back on the shelf.

I took a breath. Okay. Ready to leave.

Just before I triggered the door open, I crouched down.

It saved my life.

The plasma blast soared over my head, singeing the two inch long hair. The smell of burnt hair filled the air.

And pissed me off.

In front of me stood a big, barrel-shaped guy in black coveralls, clutching a laz-pistol in one hand.

Stupid. Those things were notoriously front heavy.

I tucked my chin to my chest and lunged forward. My head caught him in the diaphragm. I heard a loud oof.

At the same time, I yanked my left arm up. Knocked his forearm.

The laz-pistol went flying.

I stomped on his foot but he was wearing heavy space boots. Still, it was a slight distraction.

He was still gasping for breath as I reared back. Palm up, I swung. Arm, shoulder, body all in.

And hit him on the side of the face. I almost felt his cheekbone crunch under the force of my blow.

His head snapped back. Eyes rolled upward.

I finished him with a solid uppercut. His teeth clicked together.

He fell backward like a collapsing temporary lifepod, all shrivelled and spent.

I stood over him, panting hard, rubbing my bruised knuckles

and willing my galloping heart beat to slow. When it felt like I could stoop without passing out, I bent over him, running a fast search.

A first pat down didn't yield anything, not even the requisite station ID. If he'd been caught by security without it, that was five days in lockup. That was one thing about my ex, he took regulations seriously.

It could be this thug had left everything behind on his way to get here but something told me it wasn't quite so simple. Had he been tasked to shoot anyone who came out of RJ's room or me specifically? I'd never seen this guy before and it was a good bet he'd never seen me, so he'd had to have something on him to let him identify me.

I had to search again. This time a little more thoroughly.

I pulled a slim scanner from my pocket. About as thick as my thumb and almost six inches long, when pointed at anything, it projected a holographic display as it scanned the object in focus. It was highly illegal and just one of the tools I had that my ex would have had a fit over.

What he didn't know wouldn't hurt me.

I traced the scanner over the thug, paying special attention to the seams and hems of his clothing. If there was a hidden pocket or something hidden in the fabric, it would probably be there.

The scanner blinked when I reached the waist.

There, tucked into a fold on the right, a tiny holo projector, a black, round wafer, the size of my pinkie nail. Enough memory to project a single image. I tapped the side where the trigger button was and it turned on. Not even bio locked. Either they were sloppy or they didn't care who saw the image.

Dim light sprang up from the top of the holo projector. After a moment, the image solidified.

Me.

Great.

I turned off the projector and shoved it into my pants pocket. Then I continued scanning the thug. As I expected, I didn't find anything else.

When I finished, I tucked my scanner back into its hiding place in my belt. The book had slipped out of my jacket and ended up on the floor. I picked it up, keeping an eye on the thug. He showed no sign of waking.

The laz-pistol had ended up several feet away. I debated taking it. It would be nice to be armed, especially since someone was specifically targeting me, but that laz-pistol was bulky and not well-balanced. I could do better.

I backed away down the hall, keeping an eye on the thug just in case. At the end junket, I paused and placed a call to security. Code alpha red. Imminent danger to the station. My ex would be pissed when he found it was my call signature, but finding someone flaunting the regulation about carrying ID and weapons might soften his stance.

I hurried away before security could arrive.

3

I had to assume my office was being watched. It wouldn't be useful to me at the moment, but I was going to miss Robby. Still, I couldn't risk going back. Not yet. I had to find another place to lie low.

Fortunately, I had a few options.

I headed to O level, more crowded than T level, but that just allowed me to blend into the crowd. There, three doors from the lift junction was Melba's Midnight Oasis. Instead of the normal, steel-grey, she'd had the double doors painted a deep, midnight blue, with carved lines curving upward toward the stylized letters that pulsed in a deep glow above the doors.

I'd always thought it was a silly name for a brothel on a space station where there was no real midnight but Melba liked the exotic sound of the name.

One of the three licensed brothels on the station, I had met Melba years ago when some scammer had targeted several of her clients. Although she wanted to protect their identity, she refused to allow the blackmail to continue. She'd cooperated with a security sting and still managed to protect her clients. She was tough, sensible, and might just be willing to extend me some help, if it didn't compromise her.

I hoped whoever was hunting me didn't know about her.

I spent a few minutes huddled in an alcove a few doors down and across the way. I had to keep my head down as I studied the crowd.

It was the only time I regretted keeping my hair shaved short. Nothing to hide behind.

But I managed to tilt my head in such a way that it didn't look like I was watching the crowd. After a few minutes, I was satisfied that no one but me was surveilling Melba's Midnight Oasis.

I slouched out of the alcove and ducked through the crowd toward those carved doors.

And spotted a twin to the thug I'd taken down just a short while ago.

Similar black coveralls. Similar no-neck look as his head seemed to melt down into his shoulders. This guy had spiky black hair and a somewhat scruffy goatee. The only thing he was missing was the laz-pistol but only an idiot would carry one of those in a crowd. That would practically guarantee a take-down by security.

Hmm.

For a moment, I regretted not grabbing laz-pistol from the thug number one. Maybe I could have planted it on thug number two.

But did I need the actual laz-pistol?

I ran a finger along my belt, felt the slight bump of my slim scanner. It didn't just scan, I knew, it could also display.

All I needed was to get a little closer for what I had in mind. Oh, and not be seen of course.

A cluster of four people sauntered by. They have the look of tourists to them. Bright, new clothing, shiny shoes, hair coiffed in flowing, bobbing coils on their heads. They managed to take up almost the entire width of the corridor.

And they were heading right toward thug number two.

Perfect cover.

I slipped in behind, shuffling along, closer to the wall. Even with their cover, I couldn't assume they'd walk all the way down. Being doubly careful had saved my butt many a time.

Sure enough, they started to turn into a restaurant still four doors shy of reaching thug number two. If I was going to attempt this, it would have to be soon.

I slipped the slim scanner out of my belt. A few taps took it from scan to display mode. As the final tourist sauntered through the restaurant door, I aimed the scanner and hit the button.

Across the hall, two doors down half hidden in shadows, a duplicate of me appeared. I had it turn its head right and then left before stepping toward the middle of the hall.

Surely thug two couldn't miss it.

And he didn't.

Instead of producing another laz-pistol, thug two was a little subtler. He let his hand drop down to his side. Only because I was watching so closely did I notice the thin, silver blade of a whisper knife.

Damn, he wouldn't be noticable in the crowd with that thing.

I was going to have to do something more drastic.

I cupped my hand around my mouth, turned my head to the right.

"He's got a knife," I yelled.

The crowd froze. The urge to dart away made me itch, but if I moved, I'd be completely noticeable. As it was, thug two's startled expression and jerking of his head made him the focus of the crowd.

Someone screamed.

The crowd lunged like an animal. People scattered, running into each other or around each other. A siren began to bellow.

In the mayhem, thug two darted forward, knife out. He swiped toward my holo display.

I had to admire his dedication to his job. Even in this total mess, he was still following orders.

You just didn't see that kind of work ethic anymore.

The knife blade slid right through the centre of the holo display.

The shock on thug two's face was a thing of beauty. Right before several security guards emerged from the end of the hall and slammed him to the ground.

Somehow he still managed to hold onto the knife. Would have been smarter to let it go, try to claim it wasn't him. Security tapes would prove him wrong but he could have bought himself some time.

Maybe thug two wasn't as smart as I'd thought.

As the crowd scurried away from the scene, I let it drag me along. When I spotted the carved doors of Melba's Midnight Oasis, I slid up to them and then darted inside.

As they clicked closed behind me, the blare of the siren cut off, leaving only the calm, soothing music that tinkled in the air. I breathed in the smell of eucalyptus.

The waiting area stretched out before me. Long, low couches lined the walls. Rich tapestries of dark red, rich purples and deep blues covered the space above them. Gauzy fabric draped from the ceiling, diffusing the light. Pillows were everywhere. Smaller ones dotted the couches, larger ones sat on the floor, half covering the ornate throw rugs.

Floor length curtains covered the far wall. The centre parted and a woman emerged. Her body was covered in a golden glow that rippled along her muscles as she walked. A single piece of deep gold fabric was draped over her left shoulder, flowing down to cover her breasts and torso before rippling to the floor. It had the look of a golden water fall flowing over her.

"Welcome to Melba's Midnight Oasis." Her voice was a deep throaty purr, one that I imagined she regulated to whatever the client liked. "We cater to all."

That wasn't quite true. I knew of several more extreme fetishes that Melba refused to indulge. But most of those were lethal. Melba was very protective of her employees. I'd even heard that she had refused the ReProg for the longest time, until it was deemed safe by the Planetary Alliance health services. ReProg allowed someone to write over their own personality, for a limited time. To literally become someone else. Once Melba had allowed it, even if the client requested a reprogram, Melba ensured the employee could break it at any time if they needed to. It had been a real novelty for a while but it was really more useful for intelligence operatives.

Someone like RJ.

"I need to talk to Melba," I said.

Maybe it was something in my tone. The woman's demeanor shifted slightly, drawing away from me. She nodded and retreated back behind the curtain.

A moment later the curtain parted again and this time, Melba stepped through.

Even in heels, Melba barely came up to my shoulder. Her long, black hair was pulled back to the nape of her neck with a silver clip. She wore a black tunic over black pants, the fabric stretching over her somewhat heavy bulk. Her eyebrow arched at the sight of me and she crossed her arms across her ample chest.

"Let me guess," she said. "You need work."

"I've got work," I said. "I need a place to lie low for a short time."

I told her everything. I knew better than to try to lie to Melba. She'd sniff it out faster than an oxygen leak in the storage hold. Plus with her steady supply of customers, she might have heard something useful.

Something about RJ or maybe even Claymore.

But when I finished, she shook her head.

"I haven't heard anything about any of this," she said. "I haven't had any client named RJ or Claymore."

"How about someone interested in books?" I asked. "Maybe someone carrying books with them?"

Melba tapped a finger on her chin. With each tap, the short nail on her finger shifted hues, starting from a pale pink and deepening with each tap.

"You mean like a librarian fetish?" she asked. "We have one guy who likes to pretend he returns research material late and needs to be punished."

I shook my head. "Nothing like that. Maybe someone who talks about them or carries one around."

"No, sorry."

I sighed. I could still feel the Stephen King book pressing against my rib cage under my jacket. Should I show it to Melba? Would that put her into even more danger than just giving me a place to hide for the moment?

Better not risk it. If somehow someone had noticed me slipping in here they might question Melba. What she didn't know, she couldn't give away and she wouldn't have to hide it either. It was bad enough that I'd spilled everything to her so far, I didn't have to get her in any deeper.

"Do you have an untraceable terminal I can use?" I asked.

Her lips pursed. Her eyes narrowed.

"You took one of those books you mentioned," she said.

I didn't response. My heart started to pound. Was she going to insist on seeing it? Would I have to dart out of here?

"And you aren't going to show me," she said. She let out a sigh. "You don't have to protect me, girl. I've been around a lot longer than you."

"Maybe I don't want to share my commission," I said.

She laughed. "Right. Money is so important to you. That's why you barely squeak along while insisting on helping people who can barely afford you."

"I do all right," I said and managed to not wince at the whining quality in my voice.

A smile bloomed on Melba's face. "Don't get me wrong, girl, I'm a sucker for a white knight. Not too many around in these cynical times."

"I'm no white knight," I said.

Her smile widened. "You keep telling yourself that, girl." She beckoned me toward the curtain. "Come on, I'll set you up."

I wanted to argue, tell her I wasn't out to save anyone, just my own hide, but she slipped through the curtains, leaving me to protest to the empty waiting room.

I sighed. Did it matter what she believed? As long as I got a chance to try to figure out what this book said and how I was going to get myself out of this mess.

Fussing with the curtain, I managed to find the split and pushed my way through. A long hall stretched off before me with closed doors lining the way on either side. No sound emanated from within although I knew Melba had microphones and videos hooked up to every room. She claimed not to record anything and only used it to ensure the safety of her workers. There'd never been any complaints about her practices to station security as far as I knew so maybe Melba was telling the truth about not recording.

But who knew?

I knew better than to ask.

Melba was already all the way down the hall. She gestured at me. I hurried forward, my shoes making soft tapping sounds against the mental floor. But even that sounded hushed in the hallway, like the sound was deadened, although with the complete nothing coming from the doors I passed.

It was kind of creepy.

"I sound proofed the hallway," Melba said. "That is why it is so silent."

"I didn't ask," I said.

"No, but your face is all pinched up like a prune."

"It is not," I said.

A hint of a smile curled the corner of her lips. She patted my left cheek.

"Of course not. There's a terminal in here."

The door before her slid open. The room was barely larger than a closet. A screen was inset into the wall with a ledge underneath. Melba pressed her palm to the centre of the ledge. Lights flickered and an illuminated keyboard appeared.

"My bookkeeper uses this terminal to download our receipts," she said. "It has a connection to the station's network but it can be disconnected. Or you can use it in stealth mode."

Naturally Melba would have an untraceable link to the network. I had always suspected as much. I was sure that security suspected it as well. Maybe one of them had even installed it for her.

"Thanks," I said.

"If you're going to connect in stealth mode, you'll only have about fifteen minutes," Melba said. "The encryption only lasts so long before the station AI breaks through."

I nodded. I knew how fast the station AI worked. It was one of the reasons I wanted an upgrade for Robby. It would have a better chance riding the datastreams than I would.

But I was going to have to give it my best now.

Melba backed out and shut the door. Now I really did feel

like I was in a closet. Or maybe a coffin. The door was barely two inches from my right arm. I barely had to move to poke it with my elbow. The air had a musty quality to it, with the stale scent of old lavender. Did the bookkeeper wear lavender?

I pulled the book out from under my jacket and flipped it open. Starting from the beginning, I paged through it. The first quarter of the book was clean. The markings didn't start until page seventy-one. I flipped through the rest quickly. Almost every page after that had markings until the last quarter of the book, then it went blank again.

Had RJ not had a chance to fill in the rest of the book or was he trying to hide the markings?

The only way to find out was to break the code.

I turned back to the beginnings of the marks. The lines and dots were crisp, sure. Made with a slim marker. The movements quick but still precise. As I turned the pages deeper into the book, I noticed that the marks looked more hurried. Lines seemed not as straight or crisp. The ink seemed thinner, the colour faded.

Like RJ had had only one writing implement and he was trying to keep from using it all up before he finished writing down his messages.

I spent another ten minutes reviewing each page, looking for some kind of pattern, something to help me start to figure it out. Even connecting to the datastream, I needed somewhere to start, something to feed into the system so it could start breaking the code.

And if I only had fifteen minutes before the AI broke through the stealth mode, the more work I could do up front the better.

The lines, dots, and squiggles seemed to swim before my eyes. The pages crinkled as I turned them. The edges caught on my nails, picked at my skin. The musty lavender stench seemed to permeate everything, making me want to gag.

I was never going to figure this out. Why was I even trying?

I turned another page. The squiggles swam in front of my eyes. I rubbed the bridge of my nose and focused again.

Wait a minute. Hadn't I see that kind of squiggle close to some similar words?

My heart started to pound as I flipped back and forth through the book, reviewing the lines and dots, matching with the closest words. It wasn't an exact correlation but it was close.

Enough to run it through the terminal and get some kind of result before the AI broke through.

I opened the connection and entered in ten of the most common markings, along with the words and phrases adjoining them. Then I set it to break the code.

Minutes seemed to stretch on. My mouth felt dry and stale with the lingering taste of old coffee. It mingled with the lavender stench. The stool under me dug into my butt. The walls seemed to press even closer. At least the ceiling of the tiny room was high above me, but instead of being comforting, it just made the room feel narrower.

Why was this taking so long? Was the stealth connection compromised? Had someone set up a program to catch these symbols and word phrases? Had I betrayed Melba? Was security or someone else already on the way?

I felt my breath quicken. My heart pound. Adrenaline made me fidgety.

Settle down. Breathe. Being paranoid wasn't going to make the computer work faster.

But being paranoid had saved my life before.

Was it saving me now?

I didn't have a time piece but the log on the computer ticked over to ten minutes. Still working. Only five minutes left in the stealth connection before the AI broke through.

Theoretically.

It could probably break through even sooner, especially if it sensed something inherently dangerous about the code I was trying to crack.

The timer ticked off another minute. The flashing symbols on the screen still look impenetrable.

It wasn't going to break it in time. I had to pull the plug.

My hand shook a little as I reached for the off switch. Another minute ticked by.

Now only three minutes left.

I strained to hear anything beyond the door but Melba's soundproofing in the hall was too good. If security was already breaking in, I wouldn't hear them until they were on top of me.

Until it was too late.

Another minute.

Two left.

I had to shut this down. I had to. It wasn't working.

Whatever code RJ was using, I hadn't been able to find enough common ground for the computer to figure the rest out.

I needed to stop it.

Why couldn't I stop it?

My hand shook even harder. Hovering over the disconnect button.

Another minute ticked by.

One more left.

My blood roared in my ears. My heart beat so hard in my chest it made the muscles ache.

The timer flashed in the bottom left corner of the screen. Counting down from thirty. Twenty-nine, twenty-eight...

Too late. I had to shut it down.

Any second now the AI would break through, alert security, if it hadn't already.

Fifteen, fourteen, thirteen...

The symbols stopped flashing. They shifted. Reconfigured.

Into numbers.

Numbers that looked vaguely familiar.

Seven, six, five...

I slammed my fist down on the cut off the button.

The screen froze. Before it died completely, I pulled out my thin scanner and plugged it into the access port on the side of the screen. It took a quick snapshot of the information. Then the connection closed. The screen dimmed.

I pulled the scanner out of the port and sagged back against the chair. I felt like I'd run a marathon. My body felt slick with sweat. The stink of my anxiety filled the little room. At least it overpowered the horrid lavender.

I tucked the scanner back into the little pouch at my waist. I then closed the book and slipped it back inside my jacket although I didn't think I needed it anymore.

Good to keep it though, just in case.

Especially since I recognized those numbers.

Case files.

Station security case files.

Confidential. Classified.

How had RJ found them? What cases did they pertain to?

What did it mean?

I didn't want to know. I wanted to rewind this day. Go all the way back to the beginning. Instead of being home when Claymore arrived, I wanted to head out off to O level for breakfast. Maybe he wouldn't have come back. Maybe I wouldn't have taken his case. Maybe I wouldn't be in this mess.

But there was no way back and even if I wanted to give it up,

I somehow didn't think it would matter to the thugs that were after me.

Too late to back out now. And with my reputation, no one would believe it anyway.

Damn my own pride in a job well done.

Why couldn't I have slacked off on the occasional job before this?

Enough self-pity. I had to move. I couldn't stay in Melba's any longer.

Especially not holding onto a scanner full of station security case file numbers.

I stood and shuffled around the seat to the door. There wasn't much space, I still felt the press of the chair against the backs of my legs. I opened the door and peered out.

The hallway was empty.

So far so good.

Maybe the AI hadn't detected anything abnormal.

Maybe my luck was holding, for the moment.

I stepped out into the hallway, triggering the door to close behind me.

A muffled thump sounded at the far end. The door leading back to the waiting area.

Oh crap.

Melba appeared at the other end. She grabbed my arm and yanked me farther down the hall.

"Hurry, they're coming," she said. "The door won't hold for long."

She led me to the end of the corridor. The back door opened into a luxurious office. Thick pattern rugs covered the metal floor. Rich, burgundy and purple tapestries covered the walls. I was barely able to glance at them but I was sure those multiple figures were doing some pretty, um, intense things.

A louder thump sounded, followed by a screech of metal.

Melba pointed toward the wall behind her desk. It was a heavy, oak thing with massive carved legs that looked like lions roaring. How had she gotten that on a space station?

No time to ask. I hurried around the edge the desk toward where she'd pointed.

A tapestry hung over the wall but when Melba lifted it, I saw several squares cut into the metal platting of the wall.

"The middle one," Melba said. "Push on the left side."

I did as she said. The square shifted and swung open. I caught a whiff of machine oil and dust.

Only darkness beyond.

But I had no choice. It was either that or face security.

I bent down and crawled into the hole.

I could see a few feet in front of me in the shaft. Metal walls pressed close on either side. My scalp bumped the roof if I lifted my head an inch. Dust coated the metal floor.

I'd crawled several feet in when Melba reset the door behind me, closing off the light source, plunging me into darkness.

Pitch dark.

I froze. I wasn't really claustrophobic or afraid of the dark, but putting them both together and I could feel the walls closing in on me. Or something crawling toward me from farther along the shaft. Just my imagination, I knew, but my body was already tensing. The dust and oily smell mingled with my own sweat stench. My heart pounded. My palms felt slick pressed against the metal floor. I was sure the sides of the shaft were starting to squish my shoulders even though it had been more than wide enough when I crawled in.

Steady. Steady on. I had to have something I could use to light my way. Like most residents, I carried a variety of small emergency devices. An oxygen pouch sewn into the left sleeve of my outfit. Extra strong magnetics on the bottom of my boots in case of loss of gravity.

And a tiny pin light that could clip onto my collar.

Now where did I keep the damn thing?

I shifted back onto my haunches and lifted my hands to my body, patting along my belt. Didn't I keep it close to my scanner?

From behind me, I heard muffled voices. Deep and loud, sounding angry followed by Melba's calmer tones.

Security had broken through and were confronting Melba in her office.

Would they find the opening into this shaft behind her desk? Had this been pointless?

I should try to crawl away as fast as I could but would they be able to hear me? Had they brought a scanner that could detect my movements?

I felt the edges of the cylindrical pin light tucked into the left side of my belt. I pulled it out and held the slim metal body in my hand but didn't trigger it. Not yet.

I waited, not moving. Not making a sound.

Waiting.

The voices grew louder but I still couldn't make out the words. Just the tone. Angry. Threatening. Melba's voice, rising in volume as well, but defiant, getting angry herself.

Then the whine of a plasma gun. A thud of something heavy landing.

Then silence.

My breath caught in my throat.

They wouldn't have...would they?

Not Melba. Not because of me.

I felt wetness on my face. Pressed my lips tight together against the sob that tried to come out of my throat.

Damn that Claymore for walking into my office. Damn me for taking this case. Damn that RJ for leaving these books behind.

No. None of us were to blame, not even me, even though I had brought this down on Melba by coming to her for help.

The blame was on the men who pulled the trigger. I had to remember that. They weren't puppets. No one made them do it. They had shot her by choice, even if the choice went all the way back to choosing to join the security on this station.

They were going to regret those choices. I was going to make damn sure of it.

I waited a full minute, listening for anything behind me before I triggered the pin light and started moving through the tunnel.

4

One good thing about living in the dregs of Bessel Station, I knew all the low end places. Some of them I'd learned about while working security, but there were hidey holes and other hidden places that even security didn't know about.

After crawling around the tunnels behind the walls for an hour, I managed to pull myself out down in Y level, smack into the middle of ones of those hidey holes.

It looked like it had been one of the original chambers built onto the station. Welding along the creases were white with age. On the exterior wall were the remnants of an old airlock hatch. A disconnected instrument panel on the right, wires still hanging down. The outline of the metal struts that had held the airlock in place. The open space had been closed off with a thick sheet of metal that looked only slightly newer than the other walls.

The air had the stench of machine oil and soiled socks. Piles of rags were heaped into several corners. As I crawled out of the ventilation shaft near the floor, I twisted to avoid disturbing one of the piles. I knew better. One person's junk was another person's prized possessions on a space station. And they would be might pissed to have them disturbed.

Getting to stand upright felt like luxury after crawling around for so long. The vertebrae in my back snapped and crackled as I stretched. Muscles I never knew existed shrieked at their mistreatment. I spent a solid ten minutes stretching out before I felt human again.

On the final stretch, I felt the book shift under my jacket. A subtle reminder that this was not over yet.

Like I could forget.

Nothing could make me forget the sound of Melba's angry voice and the whine of the plasma gun. Or the solid thump and then silence.

Someone was going to pay for that.

I blinked away the moisture in my eyes. Focus. I had to keep moving. Had to figure out what was going on.

Had to learn what was in that classified security file from RJ's book. Had to find out how deep this went.

Even if it went all the way. All the way to my ex.

If it did, divorce would seem like a picnic compared to what I was going to do to him.

But first I had to get cleaned up. I was sure I rivaled the stench in this room. Any of the levels beyond the worst of the worst and they wouldn't need to track me. They could just follow the fumes.

Good thing a couple of my hidey holes weren't as bad as this one.

The halls in Y level were deserted, dusty, and badly lit. I still didn't linger long. I lifted my feet as I hurried along, trying not to disturb the fine layer of soot that covered the metal floor.

Lighting was dim, giving me ample shadows to hide in. Unfortunately, it also allowed others to hide as well. As I moved,

I heard the telltale shuffle of worn boot on metal grating. A metallic clink.

Warning shot.

"Passing through," I said, just loud enough to reach the spot where the metal clink had come from.

Odds were it wasn't security. Probably one of the low dwellers. Out of money and barely able to scrape by. Usually they wouldn't bother anyone unless they bothered them.

I kept moving, lifting my feet, but keeping my stance loose. Just in case.

The shuffling sound pulled away, deeper into a recess.

They didn't want trouble any more than I did.

I moved on by, making sure not to look back, even as I listened for anyone following.

No one did.

They had wanted to be sure I was just passing through.

The corridor deadended at a T junction. I turned right. As I moved along, the lighting brightened. The dust thinned. The walls looked less scratched. The metal less worn. It was still Y level but the cleaner part.

I found the out-of-the-way ladder leading to a hatch in the ceiling. Left over, just like the air lock, but this hatch was still used. It moved soundlessly as I twisted the wheel. A little tight, but it still moved. Finally I heard the click and the hatch lifted away, airing hissing, proving it still had a good seal.

Still good after over thirty years. I could say the same. Hoped I be able to say it for many years to come.

I climbed up and found myself in a deep alcove on X level.

Just a step up from Y, it had many more times the people, so navigating would be interesting. As I reset the hatch, I listened. Nothing sounded beyond the alcove entrance. The air had a slightly less dusty texture but still smelled ripe.

Or maybe that was just me.

I definitely had to get cleaned up. I wouldn't blend in much longer.

Crouching, I poked my head out. A trick I'd learned in security. Never look out at the approximate head level. Someone might be looking to shoot it off. If you looked out at a different height, it might be enough to confuse your enemy and give you time to get a shot off.

If I had any kind of weapon.

Still, it would stop me from getting my own head blown off.

And it showed me there was no one around.

At this moment, anyway.

The corridor was the same grey, unpainted metal as Y level, but with less grime, less dents, and less wires hanging around.

I slipped out and headed right, scurrying quickly down the hall. My boots made quick tapping sounds but they didn't carry.

The corridor curved and branched. I took the left and started to count my steps. Forty-four in and I came to a metal plate. It looked like all the other metal plates covering the walls. But it wasn't.

A couple of twists and I was able to pry away the bolts. The metal plate swung away. I caught the edge and climbed into the spot behind it, pulling the plate back into place. Just before my fingers got trapped, I snatched them back and grabbed the tiny handle I'd welded to the inside. The plate snapped back into place.

In the dark, I felt on the wall beside it. There, the little metal hook I'd attached. I flipped it over until it hooked onto the handle, holding the plate closed.

Now I could turn on a light without fear of being discovered.

I pressed against the wall under the hook, feeling the plastic covering over the bio-light I'd installed. After a moment, several strips of light positioned in the space began to glow.

It was the size of a small closet, wide enough for me to turn around it, but not much else. If I held out my arms, my elbows would bump the walls on either side. In the corner was a small crate that held a two day supply of expired protein bars, some energy cubes, a half stocked medi-kit, and several litres of tepid water. I really needed to swap out the water one of these days, maybe even try to replace the protein bars.

On a hook in the left corner hung a plastic garment bag holding several different outfits, complete with different ident cards and personas. Not even my ex knew about these.

And that was something I was counting on.

One should always have another person to fall back on, even if it was themselves *as* another person.

I scrounged in the medi-kit and found some disinfectant wipes. They would have to do. I also cracked open one of the litres of water. It has a slightly stale scent but wasn't slimy like I expected. As I washed my face, scrubbing off the layer of grime, several water drops landed on my tongue and although they had a little plasticky taste, it wasn't bad. Maybe it wasn't so urgent to swap them out just yet.

I striped out of my clothes and left them in a pile in the corner by the plate opening. Once I was finally air dried, I turned to the garment bag.

The first few outfits weren't quite right. But the third one, yes, it would do nicely.

I pulled out the dark blue suit. The skirt cut was just above my knees with a slit up the back. White sleeveless shirt under the tapered jacket. Spray on leggings. The high heels looked uncomfortable but I'd had them specially made with extra support and maglocks in case of gravity loss.

The blonde wig was the piece de resistance. Flowing locks that spilled over my shoulders. Parted on the left with a swish of hair curving over the right side of my face. With some quick brushes of makeup and a few well-placed appliances, it changed the shape of my head and face enough that even I didn't quite recognize myself in the mirror.

Pristance Chambers, vice president of security and relations for the Delta Corp. Completely fictitious but I'd kept up her identity well enough that it should pass a reasonably extensive scan.

Unfortunately, after this, poor Pristance's identity would probably be burned. All that work and planning gone. But that was what she was for, to let me get close to a job or let me get away. As long as she did the job, I was happy.

The mirror I had was only big enough to give me a face and shoulders look. I brushed my hands down the suit, feeling the smooth, silky material. Hidden pockets inside the jacket held my scanner but weren't big enough for the book. I didn't want to leave it behind.

I checked the garment bag. A portfolio rested at the bottom. It was for another identity but I could repurpose it. I pulled it out. It was more than big enough for the book but too narrow. I opened the sleeve. Definitely too narrow, but if I opened the book, it might just fit.

I flipped the pages until I hit the middle and slid it into the portfolio. It just fit, but enough that I could close the cover. The gaudy orange and grey design did not go with my suit. Fortunately, it was a cheap portfolio. The design was a simple holo. All I had to do was delete it, leaving the plain black surface.

Pristance Chambers was ready. I just hoped I was as well.

I climbed out of the hidey hole and hurried away. As far as I could tell, no one saw me but I had to be open to the possibility that this hole was burned. Fortunately, I still had a few others hidden around the station if necessary.

I sure hoped it wasn't necessary.

5

I felt a little wobbly in the heels, despite the cushioning and the extra magnetic locks. But by the time I reached the upper levels I had a handle on them and was able to walk more smoothly. Pristance should walk like she was born in these heels.

I kept my back straight and head up. The blonde hair bounced on my shoulders. I noticed people glancing at me. Were they operatives? Was I already blown?

Then I noticed the suggestive leer on a lounging docker's face.

Not blown, it was the Pristance persona. She was noticeable in ways that I wasn't and I wasn't used to be stared at. I decided that Pristance was used to it, but ignored it as unimportant. So I did the same.

Even with the mag locks, my heels clicked against the metal floor. I had reached L level, where the main security office was and the centre of the shopping district on the station. Unlike O level, with the restaurant mingling with higher end brothels, L level was strictly shopping. From clothing to jewelry to electronic trinkets that did little other than blink, twinkle or beep. You could get similar junk in the market stalls down on W level for a fraction of the price, but that didn't have the prestige of L level.

L level was where the ultra rich came to play, if they deemed Bessel Station worth playing on.

The metallic floor gleamed, a real trick considering the constant foot traffic. The walls were a mix of clashing colours and textures as each shop seemed to war with the other for attention. First one was lime green with a folded fan texture, the next was brilliant red like plush velvet, and the next was black and smooth as leather.

As well, subliminal messages flickered just inside the doorways, flashes of holos, light, tickling sounds and brief whiffs of aromas, all designed to entice the shopper inside. Fortunately, neither the smells or lights were too powerful to cause nausea. The shop owners knew better than to overpower their patrons with a war of smells and tastes. Vomiting, headachey shoppers weren't going to spend credits.

And there right in the middle, was the main security office, looking drab and dull in plain, gun-metal grey. Simple black lettering along the top spelled out BESSEL STATION SECURITY. Frosted glass allowed light into the offices and let the security teams look out but no one could look in, except through the plain glass in the door. But by the time you got close enough to peek inside, all of the various cameras, DNA snoopers, and breathalyzers had taken enough samples of you that they already knew by a probability of eighty percent what your request was before you finished strolling through the doorway.

If there was one thing my ex loved, it was the latest gimmicks in reading pheromones, moods, DNA, and so on. Anything to do the work for him so he didn't have to develop his own ability to read people.

Despite her sophisticated look, there was no way Pristance

Chambers would make it past all those detections without betraying me. I would have to get in to the security offices another way.

Fortunately, I knew where the side door was and how to get through it.

A simple distraction holo hid the narrow opening of the alley that ran between the security office and the clothier next door.

I wandered closer to the window of the clothier, pretending to study the rotating sparkly top that hovered at eye level. It stopped when I got close enough for the window sensors to sense me. Instantly, the top shifted into a brighter blue colour, as if trying to find a version that would appeal to me. I gave a slight shake of the head. Pristance wouldn't like something so gaudy. Instantly the colour shifted, getting darker, more subdued. The sparkles faded. It actually didn't look too bad now, even with the halter and low cut.

I tilted my head, pretending to consider it, as I shifted back onto my right foot. I let my hair fall over my shoulder as I glanced around.

No one was looking my way.

I back pedaled three steps, then another two steps right and passed through the wall.

The energy of the holo tickled the hairs on my neck as I passed through. After the bright wildness of colour of light in the main corridor, it took a moment for my eyes to adjust. The alley between the shop and the security office was dimly lit, just enough to avoid bumping into the walls. Any more light would ruin the illusion of the false wall at my back.

Although there weren't any sophisticated pheromone readers here, I knew there was a camera sensor that had triggered as soon as I passed through the holo field. If I hesitated, someone inside would notice. I had to make it look like I belonged here.

Fortunately, the security team was large enough that not everyone knew everyone else. I might be able to parlay that into sneaking my way in.

As long as I didn't run into anyone I knew well.

I sure hoped Pristance Chambers would hold up.

I moved down the alley like I belonged there, trailing one hand against the smooth metal wall on the left. Twenty feet in was the door to the security office. A simple metal door with a simple card key for admittance.

Now came the tricky part.

I didn't actually have a card key any more.

I had never been good about keeping my card key on my person. It was just one more thing that I had to try to keep track of and my constant misplacement of it was one of the things that had driven my ex crazy. So much so that he had installed a hidden finger print access just for me so he wouldn't have to put up with me constantly breaking in through the door.

I was betting he'd forgotten all about it in the interval since our divorce and why not? No one else had needed access that way.

My mouth tasted sour as I let my fingers traced the wall beneath the card reader. There had been a small indent just below it that I needed to press to activate the finger print reader. If my ex hadn't disabled or removed it, the indent should still be there.

Where was it?

Seconds seemed to tick away. I could feel sweat start to soak into the jacket. This was taking too long.

Any minute now someone was going to notice that I wasn't coming in through the side door. They would wonder about that.

And decide to investigate. I would be blown.

Come *on!*

My thumb nail snagged on something three inches down from the card reader. Was it that far down?

Yes! I could feel the slight indent of the reader, the cool metallic feel. I pressed my thumb to it.

Nothing happened.

Dammit. Had my ex remembered this after all? Had he disabled it?

Was a team already assembling to take me down?

My heart pounded so hard I was sure it was fluttering my jacket. It felt like I'd been standing out here for hours when it was probably only a few seconds.

I hoped.

Try one more time. Maybe some dirt had infiltrated the delicate mechanism. I tugged on the jacket sleeve, used it to wipe at the spot on the wall.

I found the metal spot again. Pressed my thumb against it. A little harder this time.

Was it my imagination or did the metal plate feel a little warmer?

A soft click sounded. The door slid open in front of me.

I wanted to sag with relief. But I couldn't Pristance Chambers would never sag.

I stepped into the security offices. The last place I thought I would ever be again.

The interior looked the same as always. The same dull grey walls. The darker grey carpeting that absorbed sound and was easily washable in case any of the 'patrons' had an accident. Not that my ex put up with a lot of head busting but vomiting from excessive stimulants was not unknown.

As such, the air always held a slight undercurrent of

ammonia from the constant cleaning. I noticed it the moment I stepped through the door but after a breath or two, it faded.

Funny how the senses acclimatized so quickly again. It was the oddest déjà vu.

Along with the familiar smells was the familiar background hum of almost constant chatter. People at the front desk, officers responding to questions over comlinks, interrogations, reports. Most at a quiet level but punctuated by the occasional yell of a disgruntled perp.

Case files were kept in the back, away from the front area, offices, and interrogation rooms. It was going to be quite the gauntlet to run.

Better get started.

I squared my shoulders and took the first left, heading deeper into the offices.

I kept my gaze straight ahead as I passed cubicles and stations. I felt the occasional curious glance but no one said anything. If I caught someone's eye I gave a noncommittal nod. They always nodded back in acknowledgment and then looked a little smug at the questioning looks from the other officers. Yeah, sure, they knew who the hot blonde was, of course.

Yeah right.

They all assumed I was on another shift, or deep under cover. As long as I moved with purpose, no one would question me.

I passed the last row of open cubicles. Then there was just the chief's office on the right and the case file data room straight ahead.

Almost there.

The door to the security chief's office slid open.

My ex stepped out.

He looked much the same. Dark hair cropped short to his squarish head but there was a little bit of white at the temples now. A few more wrinkles at the corners of his brown eyes. But no corresponding gut protruded from his uniform. Instead, he looked as fit and trim as ever. I had a sudden recall of his body without the grey uniform, sweat glistening on broad shoulders, the feel of his rough-skinned hands.

Damn. I pushed the image away. The physical had never been our problem. It had always been when we started to open our mouths to talk.

Now if I could only move by without talking.

But unfortunately, I'd chosen a persona to hide in that stood out. And there was no way my ex would let a hot blonde walk on by without saying hello.

His eyes widened the slightest bit and he took a breath, puffing his chest up a little. I steeled myself. Would I be able to fake an accent? Would a noncommittal grunt do?

A clerk in a light grey outfit darted up. "Chief, your appointment is here." The clerk gave a jerk of his head back toward the front counter. Distracted, my ex glanced away.

I took the opportunity to increase my speed and slipped on by.

Instead of going straight into the case files, I turned left around the corner. Better to get out of sight.

"Yeah, okay," my ex said. "Send them back." His voice sounded unnaturally flat, almost bored, but I knew better. He always sounded like that when he was annoyed.

Was he annoyed that he'd missed chatting up the hot blonde? If he'd only known, he would be glad he missed that chance. Maybe he was annoyed at the meeting. I knew he didn't much like the glad-handing that went along with the security chief job.

It didn't really matter. I needed to get to the files. My ex's work life didn't matter as long as he stayed out of my way.

So naturally, I peeked around the corner.

And spotted two thugs heading into his office, looking suspiciously similar to the ones chasing me.

My stomach clenched. It was suddenly hard to breathe. My heart thudded in my chest. The fake nails on my fingers dug into my palms as I clenched my hands. The handle of the case pinched my fingers.

Son of a...

I'd always thought we'd had a cordial relationship. Mutual respect and keeping the hell out of each other's ways. How had I read it so wrong?

My ex turned to follow the two thugs into his office. His lips were pressed tight together. The tiny line between his eyebrows was deeper than usual. Definite signs of anger and annoyance.

Was he angry that they'd missed me or was he angry that he had to deal with them?

I had to know.

I took a breath. Settle down. I still had a case. I had to think. Not let myself get carried away. It would be too easy to let the fear, the grief, the anger hold sway. I had to figure out what was going on.

That meant checking those case files and finding out what they had to do with the book. Then I could find out what was going on with my ex and those thugs.

Right. I had already paid too high a price to get to this point. I couldn't lose my head now.

The case file room had the same locking mechanism as the side door. If my ex hadn't bothered to change that...

The door clicked and slid open as I pressed my thumb to the side of the card reader.

Excellent.

I stepped through the doorway, felt the tingle of the electrical scanner. The air was crisp and cool, almost cold. Better for preserving evidence and the integrity of the file storage.

To the left was the evidence storage. Rows upon rows of metal shelving filled with boxes of evidence. As per station regulations, the physical evidence was kept intact for five years before it was fully scanned and integrated into the files. That five year buffer meant a lot of space was needed to store everything from burglary tools, to weapons stashes and more.

In contrast, the file storage on the right was a single flat rectangle embedded into the wall. About the size of an extra large pizza box and twice the depth, the greyish surface was flat and unremarkable. A single light blinked at the top, showing the health of the file system. Beneath the file box, a row of three terminals sat empty.

Most active files were accessible to officers at their desks. It was only when the file was closed or restricted that anyone needed to come into the case file room to access it.

I selected the terminal on the far left. From this angle, I wouldn't be seen right away if someone came in through the door. It might give me a few precious seconds to finish.

Even with the stringent ventilation, a thin layer of dust covered the keys. As soon as I touched them, the screen in front of flickered on. The silver, grey and dark blue of the Bessel Station security logo shown out, requesting login information.

Here's where it got really tricky.

I could hack in but as soon as I started, alarms would begin ringing. I would have maybe a few seconds to shut them down before officers swarmed the room. If I managed to shut them down, no one would bother to check. I knew how often there were false alarms in the system. An alarm cutting off after a few seconds wouldn't draw attention, unless there was keener in the bunch.

But if I couldn't shut it off, I would be caught.

The cool air didn't feel so cool anymore. I found myself

sweating in Pristance Chambers's posh clothing. That wasn't good for my cover either.

I flexed my fingers. Okay, I needed to be fast and nimble for this hack.

I rested my fingers on the keys, stared at the flashing cursor in the login field.

Could it be possible?

No, not at all. Could it?

I mean, I could possibly see how my ex might forget to remove my thumb print access, especially since no one else needed it.

But surely he would have removed my security clearance for the case files.

Surely he would.

Wouldn't he?

My heart pounded. I had only one shot. I could either go for a straight hack or try to log in with my old credentials. If my old credentials didn't work, I wouldn't have time for a hack. If I started the hack, I wouldn't have time to stop and try my old credentials.

One or the other.

Choose.

Dammit. I hated making choices like this. It was as bad as when my ex tried to force me to choose what to get for take out.

I had to do something. I couldn't sit here forever.

The air tasted sour. The jacket was bunching against my back. The leggings made my legs itch. My toes ached in the high heeled shoes.

Quit whining and choose.

I pounded my fingers on the keys.

My login credentials appeared on the screen. At the end, the cursor blinked, waiting for me to press enter.

Last chance.

Screw it.

I hit the button.

The screen went grey. The little cursor flickered then the case file search screen appeared.

No alarms. No lock out.

Just a regular login.

My heart pounded. This couldn't be a mistake. For all his flaws, there was no way my ex would have forgotten to delete my access. He'd left it in, on purpose.

Why?

My mouth felt as dry as a ventilation shaft. In case there was something I could do that he was unable to, because of his position.

Maybe something like investigating RJ's disappearance.

My hands shook a little as I unclasped the case and pulled out the book. If this corruption extended into the security office and even higher, my ex might have his hands tied as to what he could do about it.

But I was outside the system. I didn't have those official restrictions. But I didn't have any official protection either.

Access was as much as he could do for me.

I had to make the best of it.

I plugged in my little scanner and then entered in the case file number. The screen flicker as it searched. My slim scanner blocked any traceware, any alarm that my search might have trigger. Still, I knew I didn't have much time. I had to get the information and get out of here as fast as I could.

I didn't want to compromise my ex any more than I already had.

Did anyone else know that he'd left me in the system? It wouldn't be that hard to find. If an investigation was conducted, it would land on him in an instant. If he'd also tried to conceal my enabled access, that would be even more damning. He might be able to plead negligence if my access was plain to see, but any attempt to conceal it would doom him.

I couldn't give anyone any reason to investigate him. No one could suspect that I'd been looking at the case files.

The light on my scanner flickered. Done. I should grab it and get out, now, before anyone decided to peek into the case file storage room.

But I couldn't help myself. I had to take a look. Just one small look.

My ex had compromised himself for this, Melba had died for this.

I opened the file.

It was encoded, of course, but I found the key easily in the opening pages of the Stephen King book. The symbols flickered and cleared.

And I read.

A human trafficking ring, but more than that. Someone was using ReProg to wipe out people's personalities and replace them with whatever the client wanted.

But not an overlay. Not something temporary. Permanent erasure, effectively killing the person who they had been, leaving only the meat suit behind to be filled up with whatever compliant personality was requested.

This was the lead RJ had been tracking. One with tentacles that stretched high into the PA ranks.

Power corrupting.

My stomach churned. I felt like I was going to vomit on the terminal.

No wonder my ex had left my credentials intact. Even if he didn't know exactly what was going on, he knew something was happening. The evidence was all over this file. Uninspected cargo holds with excess oxygen intake, a definite sign of human habitation when cargo holds were supposed to be kept in vacuum. Documentation requests refused from higher up the chain, with orders to mark certain ships as cleared without inspection.

Whoever was doing this wasn't even bothering to hide it that well. Any security officer with half a brain would notice the discrepancies.

I closed the file, making sure the copy was complete on my scanner. I was ready to go now.

But then I had a thought. I checked the security human resources files.

And found exactly why security was letting this happen under their noses.

Pay rates that were double, sometimes triple the regular amount. Even my ex's pay was double. But I knew him, he was probably banking the excess without spending any of it. If an investigation uncovered the corruption, he'd be ready to give it back in a heart beat.

I took a snapshot of the pay files, saved it to the scanner.

Now I could go.

I unplugged the scanner and tucked it back into my waist pocket, then reset the terminal. This, along with the codes in the Stephen King book, was enough evidence to break this ring wide open. Assuming I could find someone that wasn't involved in it.

This was why Claymore had come to me. No, this was why Claymore had been *told* to come to me.

And I had a pretty good idea of who had instructed him.

The least I could do was cover some of his tracks.

I turned back to the terminal and started typing. A few lines of code and I destroyed my old login credentials, back dating it to my resignation date. Not only would no one know I'd been inside the system, but no one would know my credentials had been left valid.

My heels clicked on the floor as I headed toward the door. I was halfway down the aisle when I heard the click of the door sliding open. The telltale hiss of pressure and climate being interrupted.

Someone had come in.

"Access terminals are over here." My ex's voice sounded a little grumbly, the way he'd always sounded when he was grumpy and annoyed.

"We'll take a look at it now." Another man's voice. No one I knew but I had a feeling it belonged to one of the two thugs.

And I was standing in the middle of the aisle.

I bent over and undid the latches on my heels before yanking them off. Without the magnetic holds, I'd be on the float if something happened to the gravity, but they made too much noise.

Hugging the shoes to my chest, I hurried back down the aisle toward the terminals. The metallic click of boots sounded behind me.

Only a few seconds before they turned that corner and spotted me.

Everything I'd done would be for nothing.

To my left at the end of the row of shelving was a small alcove. I darted toward it. Squeezing my shoulders I managed to shove myself in as far as I could. But even in this diffuse light, if anyone looked over, I would be completely visible.

I crouched, trying to make myself as small as possible. The wig shifted on my head, hanging more to the right.

I was just about to try to fix it when I saw movement out of the corner of my eye. A thug stepped in front of the alcove.

In profile, he looked a little tubbier than my first glance. Even with the heavy leather jacket and barely concealed laz-proof vest, I could see his gut pushing the boundaries of his pants. He wore a beard that hung a few inches off his chin, neatly trimmed but definitely designed to hide an extra chin or two. Thinning black hair was brushed back along his skull, serving only to highlight a dent just behind his ear.

He gave a nod toward the terminals. "Let's check it."

An answering grunt came from the second thug as he stepped forward. He was thinner than thug one and about a head taller. His clothing hung off him as though he had wasted away from a previously greater girth. As he reached for the keyboard, his wrist bones stuck out of the wide sleeves of his coat. His pointed chin jutted out as he regarded the keyboard and screen.

"There's no dust," he said.

"We wipe them down." My ex's voice sounded as he stepped into view. His voice sounded almost bored but I could see the tension in his shoulders. Plus I knew his ways. The more bored he could sound, the more anxious or annoyed he actually felt.

He used to sound really bored with me at times.

Thug two grunted and leaned forward to type. He didn't bother to check out the other terminals. Not the brightest then.

But you didn't need to be too bright to shoot a target squished into an alcove.

I couldn't see the screen but something on it made him frown. He stabbed at the keys again and mumbled low.

"What's that?" Thug one asked.

Thug two shook his head and kept typing and mumbling.

The cool air from the vent high above me tickled my nose. A couple of strands of blonde hair waved in front of my face but I didn't want to move to brush them aside. I felt like I could barely breathe. If not for the cold, I was sure that the stench from my anxious sweating would have reached them, although maybe they wouldn't have noticed.

But I did. My sweat made the shirt feel like it was starting to shrink and squeeze my torso. The skirt was bunched up around my knees. I hugged the shoes to my chest. I had the portfolio case tucked under my arm, hidden from view.

If they happened to look up, I figured I would have a second or two to slide the portfolio under the shelving beside me. Although I didn't know what the point would be. It wasn't like anyone would investigate my death. It would be hushed up, just like Melba's was going to be.

And the ReProg of innocents would go on.

That pierced through the icy fear that had gripped me. How many had already died trying to stop this? It had to end, and I was going to be the one to end it.

That meant I had to get out of here. Past those two thugs and past my ex.

Although I didn't have a pistol of any kind, I did have one thing going for me.

Surprise.

I tensed my body. Ready. The magnetic bottoms of my heels would do quick work on a thug's nose. Although they wore vests, they didn't have anything protecting their pants. A good knee should take care of that. Not to mention a finger in the eye.

I was perfectly fine with fighting dirty.

Thug two was still focused on the screen. Thug one was still turned toward my alcove a little too much for my liking. If he would just turn to the right a couple of inches. Just a glance.

Beyond them, my ex stood watching over thug two's shoulders. His arms were crossed over his chest. Feet slightly apart like he was on parade. Then he shifted. An inch to the left.

And lifted his gaze.

Damn.

I caught the slight widening of his eyes. A sudden jerk of a fraction of an inch as he spotted me.

I pressed my lips tight together.

Now.

I lunged out of the alcove. Slammed one shoe against the side of the head of thug two. He went down.

Second shoe smashed thug one's nose just as he turned to face me, eyes widened in surprise. He gurgled, eyes rolling up before he dropped to the floor.

Thug one was still moving. I whacked him across the face with my shoe.

Then spun to face my ex. Crouched, shoes at the ready. The blonde hair hung half in my face. I jerked my head, sending the hair back over my shoulder, so I had a better view.

My ex stood, arms still crossed. Unmoving. His pistol still holstered on his hip.

Stand-off.

Or was it?

He hadn't made a move when he could have easily stunned me. Instead he stared at me with that familiar, annoyed look on his face. His lips pressed tight together. His brows so squished, the furrow between them deepened into a crevice.

Then he jerked his head to the left.

Toward the exit.

Telling me to get out.

I stepped past the thugs and stopped at his side. The thugs were still unmoving, out cold. I could easily slip away.

But then what? My ex would be under suspicion as soon as the thugs came to.

With one smooth motion, I tucked my shoes into the curve of my right elbow and snatched up my ex's pistol. I darted back a step, raising it to point at his chest.

His mouth dropped open. The look of betrayal twisted his face.

I used the pistol to gesture to the two thugs and wiggled my eyebrows. Did he really want them to suspect him?

After a moment, the betrayal faded. He took a breath and gave a nod.

I tightened my grip on the pistol, made sure it was on stun, and shot him.

The blast knocked him back a step. For a moment, he stayed upright, then his eyes rolled back into his head and he collapsed in a heap on the floor.

Of all the times I'd wanted to shoot him when we were married, the reality of being able to do it seemed very unsatisfying.

Maybe because he didn't really deserve it after all. In truth, he wasn't a bad guy, he had just been wrong for me. Just like I was wrong for him.

We'd both known it, but at least we were able to be civil. And he could trust me to be honourable, just like I knew he was.

Maybe that's what had drawn us together in the first place.

I retreated toward the door. As I bent to put my shoes back on, I left the pistol on the floor. It was encoded to my ex and would be traceable if I tried to take it. Best to leave it behind.

Taking a deep breath, I straightened my wig and stepped out of the case file room. As the door slid shut behind me, I punched in a recalibration sequence into the lock, programming it to review security codes. The review would take about half an hour and during that time, the door would remain locked.

Hopefully it would give me enough time.

My heart pounded as I forced myself to keep a steady pace through the office. A few admiring glances followed me as I headed toward the side door but no one spoke to me. They probably assumed I was on assignment.

My hand only shook a little as I triggered the door and escaped.

6

Ten minutes later, I crammed into a fresh hidey hole behind a janitorial station on B level. Although B level had a somewhat higher level of security as it was designed station chew quarters, the reality was that it was easy to sneak onto the level as long as you looked like you belonged.

Pristance Chambers was nothing if not having the look of belonging.

I slipped my scanner into a small hand terminal and reviewed the files. Again. Hiding, squished into the hidey hole, I'd reviewed it five times already, looking for any handle I could get, any way through it.

But just like at first glance, the implications were clear.

It wasn't just the security office that was compromised. The corruption stretched all the way through the station. There was only way it could have grown like this without the Planetary Alliance become aware of it.

The governor of the station was in on it.

It didn't say as much in the files. If it came down to it, I was sure he would find a way to create plausible deniability and put everything square on the shoulders of the security chief.

My ex.

That threat had probably kept my ex in line. Until he'd figured out a way to get me on the case. Because he knew once I got my teeth into it, I would never stop.

And I sure as hell wasn't going to now. Even though it looked like Governor Gregor Milano was well insulted.

But like everything that seemed permanent, it was an illusion.

There was a way to pierce that veil. I just had to find it.

But it probably meant getting close to Governor Milano which I never would. I stiffen against the hard wall of the hidey hole.

I never would but surely Pristance Chambers could.

Good old Pristance might have a little life left in her yet. After all, she was the vice president of security and relations for the Delta Corp. And Delta Corp was maybe just thinking about opening up a new office on Bessel Station as they expanded into the quadrant.

What better reason to meet with the governor of the station?

I cleared my thought and triggered a comlink to set up an appointment for Pristance.

———

7

The governor's office was on F level, just below main station operations. Close enough to command but far enough to avoid any damage.

That seemed to be Governor Milano's motto.

The corridors on F level were the same width as the shopping concourse but without the crowds. Thick, plush, vibra-carpeting covered the metal floor, making it feel like I was walking on thick grass. The air smelled fresh and clean, with a hint of earthiness. The ceiling had been hidden by an illusion of blue sky with white, fluffy clouds floating by. It was at once an obvious show of luxury and a play to unsettle. Anyone who spent most, if not their entire, life on board a space station would find the expanse of sky above their heads to be disorienting and anxiety-producing. It was a definite attempt to put anyone off balance.

Although I knew exactly what effect the governor was going for it didn't help mitigate it. With each step across that soft, plush carpet, I could feel the wide openness of that fake sky above me.

It made me want to turn around and run back to the elevator.

But Pristance Chambers wouldn't be affected by it.

I took a deep breath, breathing in the clean, fresh air. Although it was the same air as in the rest of the station, it was definitely better filtered up here.

Power had its privileges.

Pristance would expect it and not be the least bit surprised.

Just like she would ignore the fake sky above her head. Such a gauche show of opulence would signal to her a small mind.

I allowed a slight smile to play across my lips. There was Pristance, right where I needed her.

Now I just needed her to help me get something on Milano.

The governor's office was right at the end of the corridor, a set of opulent double doors that looked like someone's fetish version of wood. They were ornately carved into a scene of trees and leaves with nubile maidens curled around the trunks, lifting apples from the branches. I wasn't quite sure what Milano was going for. Was he the snake in the garden or the benefactor?

I was sure he considered himself the later even if he was the former.

As I stepped forward, the doors slid away. From the edges, I could tell the wood was no more real than my blonde hair was. A cheap fabricated sheet that was already starting to pull away from the seal with the original metal door.

I wanted to chuckle but let Pristance's haughty look convey my disdain.

Just inside the door on the right was a large curving, marble counter top. Behind it sat a young man in a dark grey suit. Probably the security guard/receptionist.

I raised an eyebrow at him and waited.

Expectantly.

He looked back at me. I couldn't see his hands under the counter but I imagined they started to fidget under my stare.

"May I help you?" he said finally.

I lifted my eyebrow higher and tilted my head an inch to the left.

Pristance Chambers didn't announce herself. Everyone knew when she arrived.

The receptionist cleared his throat. His gaze flicked down to something on his desk below the counter.

"Ah yes, Ms Chambers, the governor is looking forward to speaking with you but he isn't quite finished with his last appointment. Would you have a seat? May I get you a coffee?"

I pulled myself even straighter, felt my spine crack a little.

"My schedule is very packed," I said, my voice cold enough to freeze the ventilation shafts above our head. "Advise the governor that I can wait five minutes past our allotted time. If he is unable to see me, I'm sure Grenier Station would be happy for my business."

With every word, the receptionist's eyes widened and he leaned away from me like I was going to reach past the counter and bite him. I allowed a slight smile to curl my lips then I spun away from him and crossed the wide waiting room in three steps. I stopped at the first chair, a Self-Chair that was even more expensive than Robby, and sat down, perching on the edge.

The receptionist turned away from me but I could see him speaking into a com, his adam's apple jumping up and down in his throat. After a moment, he finished, gave a crisp nod, and then turned back to face me.

"The governor apologizes for the wait. He can see you now."

He gestured past the edge of the desk to another set of fake wood doors.

I took my time standing up but didn't do anything that might indicate I was trying to preen before I saw the governor. Pristance Chambers didn't work to impress anyone, especially a lowly governor of a second-rate space station. She expected compliance and she got it.

I strolled across the expanse of the waiting room toward the door. The thick plush carpeting made me feel like I was teetering on the high heels. Any minute now I felt like I was going to fall over.

Pristance Chambers couldn't fall over. She knew how to walk in these heels. Too damn bad I didn't.

I made it to the doors before I fell over. My ankles trembled. My quads burned.

The faux wood doors parted and the governor stood inside. He was a few inches shorter than I was which made us the same height without my heels. His expensive, deep blue suit folded around his slightly pudgy form which was only betrayed by the thickening under his chin. Short, black hair was swept back from his squarish head. His warm smile, while perfectly professionally, still didn't reach his brown eyes which studied me over the end of his bulbous nose.

"Ms Chambers, delighted you could spare some time for me," he said as he ushered me into his office.

The plush carpeting gave way to a shorter, denser, dark brown pile that was easier to walk on. The office was larger than even the large waiting room. I could easily have fit five copies of my own office in here. To the right was a lounge area with a long couch facing three Self-Chairs. A coffee table ran the length between them and I could barely make out the seams for the inlaid monitors and controls on the smooth surface.

To the right was the governor's desk, an opulent, heavy wood desk that might actually have been real wood. I couldn't imagine the cost of transporting such a hunch of useless material up to the space station.

Lining the wall behind the desk was heavy wood shelving

filled with actual books. I had a sudden flashback to RJ's shelf and his few books. But unlike those, these leather bound volumes looked like they had never been opened.

Merely appearance, meant to impress and intimidate.

Milano took a step past me, aiming for the couch. I allowed him to take two steps before I moved toward the desk. Before he could sit, I slid into one of the Self-Chairs facing the book shelves. Seeing them made the portfolio in my hands feel heavier and I was more aware of the Stephen King book than ever.

I wondered if the governor had ever read Stephen King. He didn't look like he went in much for the classics.

The governor crossed behind his desk and sat down in the high-back, leather chair. As he did so, the arms widened and flattened. Interesting. I hadn't realized the leather chair was a Self-Chair. It must have been a much more expensive model since it mimicked a regular chair so well.

After this kind of luxury, how would I be able to return to Robby?

Although, the Self-Chair I sat in wasn't perfectly comfortable. The lumbar support poked a little too low for any good. I caught the shadow of a smirk on the governor's face. Of course he had programmed the chairs to not be perfectly comfortable. A subtle way to keep his visitors off balance.

I could have easily reprogrammed the chair, but I didn't want to give away that skill set just yet. Let the governor have his little laugh.

For now.

"As I'm sure you're aware, Delta Corp is looking to expand in this quadrant," I said. I drew the worlds out as if I'd made this pitch dozens of times. "We need a location for the regional office. Tell me why I should recommend Bessel Station to our board."

The governor launched into a glowing description of all the amenities of the station. As he talked, I slipped the portfolio onto the right arm of the Self-Chair, angling it so it hid my right hand. My thumbnail snagged onto the arm panel and I pried it open.

The governor's voice continued to drone on. I asked a few questions that propelled him into other directions.

I poked my fingers into the guts of the arm and started fiddling. After a few moments, I felt the Chair respond. First the skin became a little warmer, the shape shifted slightly under me. It settled more solidly onto the floor. The lumbar support moved to the proper spot on my back.

Good. That was as much as I would be able to do without looking. I was about to close the panel when a blinking red light caught the corner of my eye. From inside the arm.

I glanced over at the governor. He was still engrossed in his presentation, not noticing anything about my Chair.

I had to find a way to get rid of him for just a moment.

"This sounds very promising," I said. "But I find it fatiguing to discuss business with a dry mouth."

"Of course," Milano said. "How rude of me. Coffee? Tea?"

"Coffee," I said. "With a splash of something."

A smile widened the governor's face. "Of course."

He turned slightly in his Chair, murmuring the order for coffee as he reached down behind his desk.

I looked over at the arm panel.

The Self-Chair was networked with the other Chairs in the room. It was asking if I wanted to use my modifications to override the other Chairs as well.

Interesting.

I hit no and asked for a display of the network. A small graphic holo sprang up above the arm. My portfolio just hid it from the governor's view. Of course, all the Chairs in the room were slaved to the governor's own Self-Chair. He would be able to lock me in if he wanted.

Unless I managed a little tinkering.

I wouldn't be able to break the network and let this Chair become the main controller but I might be able to add another Chair to the network.

Turning off the graphic, I managed to slip my little scanner out of my waist pouch. I plugged it into the arm and set it to broadcast, linking through the station down to my little office on O level.

And Robby.

The governor pulled out a bottle of amber liquid and set it on top of his desk. I gave a very Pristance Chambers nod, regal and tilted to the right. I allowed a slight smile to curl my lips.

Milano looked pleased.

A moment later the door to the office slid open and the receptionist entered, carrying a tray with a silver pot of coffee and two white, porcelain mugs. He set the tray down on the desk and retreated, almost bowing at the door.

It clicked closed behind him.

Milano commenced pouring. "Sugar?"

"No, just black," I said. "Along with that splash."

He chuckled. "Of course."

He added a generous dollop of the amber liquid to both of our mugs before placing one in front of me.

I lifted it with my left hand and took a sip. The coffee was rich and aromatic, filling my nose with a warm, heavy scent. The flavour, strong and subtle with the bite of alcohol, danced on my tongue. It was the best cup of coffee I'd ever had, strong and rich without bitterness, and I almost moaned at the delicious taste. But Pristance Chambers wouldn't do that. The best she would do was not be disdainful.

I allowed myself a second sip before I returned the mug to

the desk. As much as I wanted to practically inhale the cup, it wouldn't do to be too enthusiastic.

Across from me, the governor sipped his coffee and placed it back down on the desk. He leaned back in his Chair and studied me. A somewhat smug expression curdled on his face.

"Now, why don't you tell me what you're really doing here?" he said.

His voice had an edge to it, one that made me distinctly uncomfortable. Would he have addressed someone of Pristance Chambers' status like that?

My shoulder blades started to itch, as if someone was aiming a pistol at my back. I resisted the urge to look around.

Instead, I raised an eyebrow and lifted my chin to regard Milano.

"What are you talking about, governor?" I asked. "I have told you Delta Corp's interest in Bessel Station."

The slight smirk deepened.

"Indeed you have, Ms Chambers." His sarcasm deepened. He unfolded his hands from in front of him and leaned back, resting his hands on the arms of his chair.

Right next to the Self-Chair controls.

"But we both know that isn't really your name," he continued. "Did you really think a cheap wig and some heels would prevent me from recognizing you? I admit it's been a while since your divorce but I always pride myself on remembering the spouses and families of my security officers."

Oh crap.

Before I could respond, he punched at the controls on the arm of his Chair. I felt my own Chair react. It deepened the seat, letting me sink into it, then tightened around me, locking me in place. The arms did the same, squeezing hard to prevent my arms from moving. No matter how much I tried, I wouldn't be able to break free.

The only part of me that wasn't locked down was my head.

The grin widened on Milano's face.

"I heard you were doing cast-off work for the security office, scraps that your ex-husband sent your way. Out of guilt or some misaligned sense of loyalty, perhaps? Is that why you thought you could help him with his investigation into my affairs? You really should have kept your nose out of it, my dear. You were smart enough to get out of a marriage with him, I don't see why you would consider sacrificing yourself now."

He shook his head. "You've caused quite a ruckus and made my associates very nervous. They were talking about moving their investment off the station. That would lose me a lot of business. But now that I've neutralized you, I'm sure they'll feel more confident. Especially after I take care of your ex-husband as well. No use having loose ends out there now, is there?" The grin faded, revealing the anger underneath. "I've had more than enough of his interference."

I felt sweat trickle down the sides of my torso, soaking into the Chair fabric around me. It wouldn't make any difference though, I still wouldn't be able to escape.

Fortunately, my fingers could still move. The panel on the right armrest was still loose. I slipped my fingers underneath, touched the smooth surface of the control buttons.

This Chair was slaved to Milano's, there wasn't any way I could disrupt that connection. But I had control of Robby and I had connected it to the network.

If I could just call up the controls.

Milano stood up from his Chair and moved around the desk. I turned my head to watch him. Would he catch a glimpse of my hand in the panel in the armrest?

But he walked toward the door, not bothering to look in my direction. Of course, I was no longer of any consequence. The

Chair had me securely in its grip. He didn't have to worry about me anymore.

Or so he thought.

I only hoped I would be able to change that.

The door slid open. I heard him call for someone and an answering murmur. As they talked, I turned my focus to the panel under my fingers. Just a few taps and I should be able to call up Robby's controls.

A moment later, a small, fuzzy holo appeared above the panel, floating in the air. The standard remote login for Robby. I entered in my master password and set it to override. The image of a clock appeared, ticking away.

I swallowed in a dry throat. The aftertaste of rich coffee had soured on my tongue. My head pounded as if from a headache from the alcohol instead of from my glaring at the floating clock.

C'mon, come *on!*

The clock disappeared and the login screen appeared again. I reentered my master password. The screen disappeared.

The air remained empty. My stomach clenched. Had I not been able to do it?

Then the activation screen appeared again, requesting my command.

I swallowed again. Now or nothing. Either my main password with Robby had overwritten Milano's control or it hadn't.

I commanded Robby to relax.

For a moment, nothing seemed to happen. Then around me, the Chair loosened. Not completely, but enough that I would be able to move, to stand.

Not a perfect override but it would do.

The voices behind me finished speaking. I heard the click of the door closing. I strained to listen but the carpeting hid the sound of footsteps. It wasn't until Milano appeared at my side that I realized he had returned.

"You've been quite an annoyance," he said. "There's only one way to get rid of that for good. I would have preferred to deal with this another way but I don't think you would listen to reason."

"I'm always willing to listen to reason," I said. "Why don't you try me?"

He tilted his head as he regarded me. A flicker of curiosity crossed his face.

"Really? You would be interested..."

I exploded out of the Chair. Milano barely had a chance to look surprised before I grabbed his arms.

He tried to yank away from me, but I could tell from the fleshiness of his limbs that he had little strength. After all, he spent his days behind a desk, talking. His jaw muscles were probably the only ones he worked out.

I spun him and slammed him down into my Chair.

"Robby, hold," I yelled.

Instantly, the Chair tightened around him. Disbelief spread across Milano's face. He struggled but the Chair held him fast.

He opened his mouth to yell. I snatched the wig off my head, wincing at the pull of it off my scalp. I jammed it into his open mouth.

He gurgled around the blonde hair.

Who said blondes have more fun?

"Robby, open secure channel to the security chief," I said.

The channel pinged. A screen appeared above the desk, unfolding and revealing my ex in his office.

"Yes, goven..."

"Code raven down," I said.

For a moment, the image of my ex froze. His lips thinned. He gave a curt nod and cut the channel.

The image of the floating screen faded back onto the bare desktop. It was also slaved to the Chair. Must be part of the upgrade. I really had to look into getting it for Robby.

Maybe after this job, I'd have enough to do it.

Somehow I had a feeling I might just be able to.

A gurgling noise sounded behind me. Milano was trying to spit out the wig. I grabbed two hunks of hair and tied it around the back of his head. His face turned red as he gurgled more. I thought he might be having trouble breathing, but no, his nose was clear. When I bent down to check, I could see the fury in his eyes.

I gave him a pat on the shoulder.

"Just you relax, governor," I said. "Security will have it all taken care of in a jiff. How about some more coffee? For me, anyway. You'll just have to wait."

I picked up my cup and refilled it from the pot. This time I didn't bother with a splash of anything else. I needed to keep my wits about me.

As I sipped the now tepid brew, I keep a close watch on the governor. As it cooled, the coffee maintained its rich flavour, transforming into something with a deeper, lingering taste. Still no bitterness.

I had a feeling the governor was not going to be the same.

How tangled was the web he'd woven, how many would be implicated? How many had he set up to take the fall like my ex? Even if we managed to mop up Bessel Station I was sure we'd miss some stragglers. Maybe even some who would be willing to extract revenge for the governor or any higher ups that would be afraid of exposure.

This was only the tip of the tail of a very ugly animal.

And when that animal was poked like this, it was liable to take a big swipe. It had already swiped hard enough to take down RJ and Melba. It wouldn't take much to erase my ex.

Or erase me.

Unless I applied a little insurance.

After all, as a single entrepreneur, I needed as much insurance as I could get.

I moved behind the desk. Old style, pull out drawers were etched into the wood. I could tell they were slaved to the same system as the Chairs. Now under Robby's control.

They opened easily.

Mostly they were full of file crystals, even some old style pads of paper.

But the bottom drawer on the right yielded something much more interesting. A small black box. It wouldn't open to my touch no matter how I pried. Then I spotted the small indentation at the front.

A thumb reader.

The governor's left thumb worked nicely. The lid popped open.

Revealing a full set of ReProg. Four ampules full of juice. The injector which looked like a pistol with a touch screen on top, ready for programming of the juice. Just plug the ampule into the injector, set the perimeters of what you want, and inject it. Usually the drug wore off after a time, but there were black market versions, the blackest of the black, that never wore off.

I lifted the injector out of the box. The silver plating gleamed in the light. It fit perfectly in my right hand. The touch screen was easy to manipulate.

"Let's see how this works," I said.

In front of me, the governor blubbered.

When my ex arrived five minutes later, the governor and I were back in our original seats. My wig was a little scruffy but still curled across my shoulders. Milano glanced up when the door slid open. He barely stopped sorting through the file crystals as he waved my ex forward.

"Come in, Chief, come in," he said. "We've got a lot of work to do. There's an illegal ReProg ring working on Bessel Station and we're going to clean it up."

My ex's brows creased in confusion. He lowered the lazer pistol he'd been holding.

"We are?" He glanced over at me. "I thought..."

"I needed to get you here without any of the others knowing," I said. "The governor asked me to call you. There's been infiltration into you office too."

"Yes, we'll have to retain your entire team, I'm afraid," Milano said. "Investigate all of them. The ones who are cleared can stay. My new head security consultant will assist you."

He gestured toward me.

My ex gaped at me.

I smiled.

I'd always hated being the underling, but being the boss, now that was something I thought I could get behind.

Plus a regular salary would definitely let me get the latest upgrade for Robby. And maybe even a better office too.

I motioned to the chair beside me.

"Take a seat, Chief. You and I can get started. This ReProg ring goes deep into PA territory and is going to take a lot of work to uncover. We'll need some coffee for this."

"I'll order a fresh pot," the governor said. He stood up and crossed to the door.

My ex stared after him, then turned back to me. I could see the questions churning through his mind, but he didn't ask them. I think he was starting to realize he didn't need to.

It wasn't about who you knew, it was about who you could ReProg.

I smiled and leaned back in the Chair. It curved around me. Not as comfortable as Robby.

But close. Very close.

ABOUT THE AUTHOR

If you enjoyed this story, please consider taking a moment to review it or to recommend it to your friends. Reviews help other readers decide if a book is for them. Sign up for the New Release Alerts so that you have first news on releases and sales: https://rebeccasenese.com/newsletter/

Based in Toronto, Canada, I write horror, science fiction and mystery/crime, often all at once in the same story. I am the author of the contemporary fantasy series, the *Noel Kringle Chronicles* featuring the son of Santa Claus working as a private detective in Toronto. Garnering an Honorable Mention in *"The Year's Best Science Fiction"* and nominated for numerous Aurora Awards, my work has appeared in *Bitter Mountain Moonlight: A Cave Creek Anthology, Promise in the Gold: A Cave Creek Anthology, Unmasked: Tales of Risk and Revelation, Obsessions: An Anthology of Original Stories, Fiction River: Visions of the Apocalypse, Fiction River: Sparks, Fiction River: Recycled Pulp, Tesseracts 16: Parnassus Unbound, Ride the Moon, Tesseracts 15: A Case of Quite Curious Tales, TransVersions, Deadbolt Magazine, On Spec, The Vampire's Crypt, Storyteller, Reflection's Edge, Future Syndicate* and *Into the Darkness*, amongst others.

Find me online:
www.RebeccaSenese.com

www.ingramcontent.com/pod-product-compliance
Lightning Source LLC
Chambersburg PA
CBHW050906180626
46814CB00007B/2918